W 81 ST
MONK'S
TAXI

In loving memory of George Shapiro and Howard West

Illustrations by Brittany Baugus
Cover design by Megan McLaughlin. Cover illustration by Brittany Baugus.

Published by Scholastic Australia in 2023.

Scholastic Australia Pty Limited
PO Box 579 Gosford NSW 2250
ABN 11 000 614 577

www.scholastic.com.au

Part of the Scholastic Group
Sydney • Auckland • New York • Toronto • London • Mexico City • New Delhi
Hong Kong • Buenos Aires • Puerto Rico

ISBN 978-1-76026-830-5

Printed in China.

Scholastic Australia's policy, in association with its printers, is to use papers that are renewable and made efficiently from wood grown in responsibly managed forests, so as to minimise its environmental footprint.

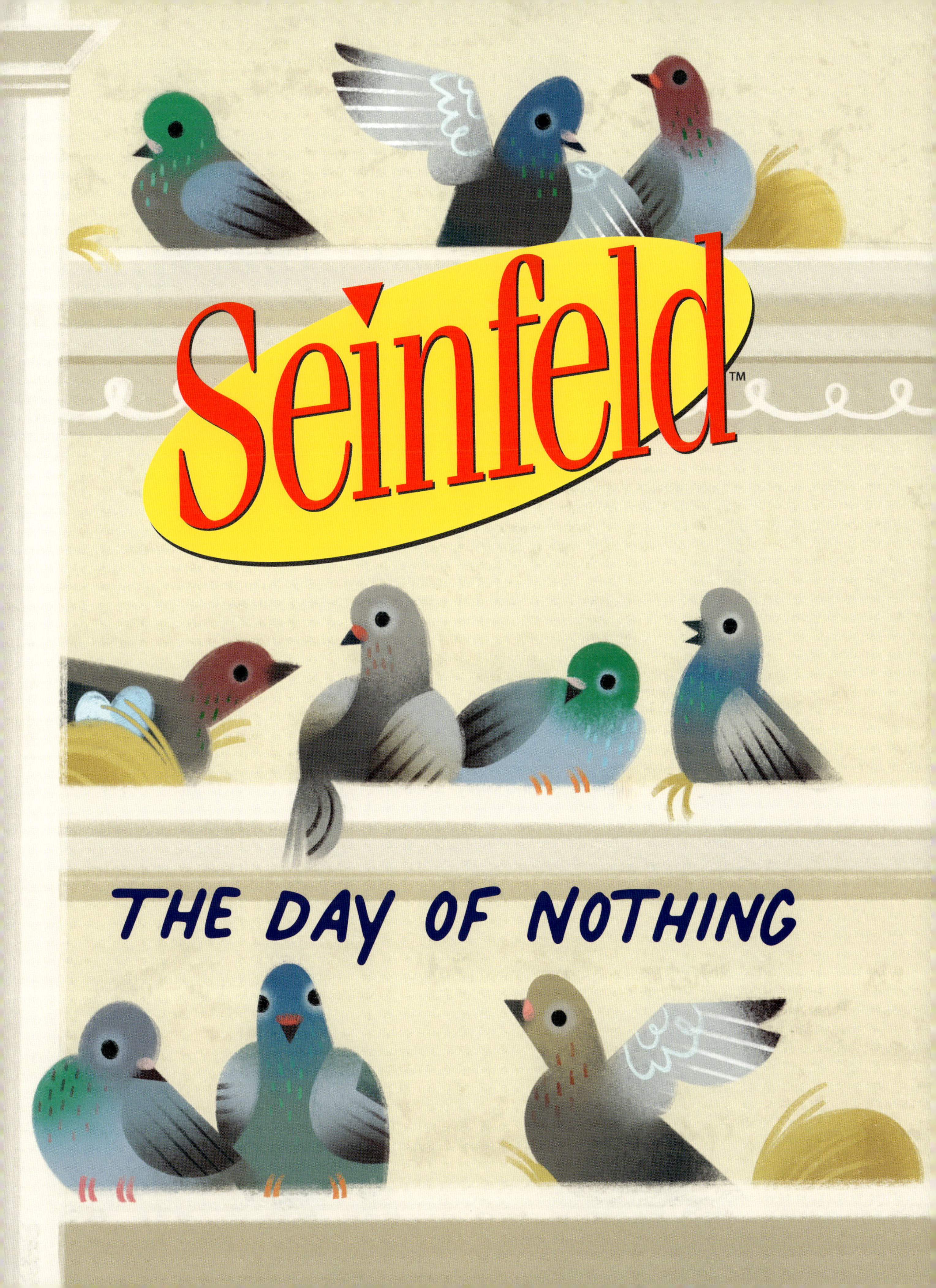
Seinfeld™
THE DAY OF NOTHING

SEARCH AND FIND

CAN YOU FIND ALL THESE THINGS AS YOU READ THE STORY?

VANDELAY INDUSTRIES

COFFEE TABLE BOOK

SUPERMAN

BLACK & WHITE COOKIE

BIG SALAD

DEL BOCA VISTA

UNCLE LEO

LOBSTER

SERENITY NOW

J PETERMAN CATALOG

FUSILI JERRY

MACKINAW PEACH

Seinfeld™

THE DAY OF NOTHING

Written by
MICOL OSTOW

Illustrated by
BRITTANY BAUGUS

SCHOLASTIC
SYDNEY AUCKLAND NEW YORK TORONTO LONDON MEXICO CITY
NEW DELHI HONG KONG BUENOS AIRES PUERTO RICO

'Did you ever notice how parents always want you to be doing *something?* They say, "Hey, it's a nice day—why don't you go outside and do *something?* What's the deal with you and your friends always sitting around, doing nothing?" I mean, what's so special about *something* anyway?'

Hi! I'm Jerry. I love baseball, Superman and eating cereal. I don't love canned fruit, my neighbour Newman or when my parents tell me to do *something*. If I have to do *anything*, you'll find me telling jokes.

‘Thanks, everyone. You’ve been a great audience. I’ll be here all week.’

With my new routine done, I had the whole day to do my favourite thing: ***NOTHING!***

But my parents had other ideas . . .

'So, Jerry, what are you doing today?' My dad asked.

'Kramer and Elaine are coming by,' I said.

'But what will you *do?'* Mum asked. She sounded worried.

'Nothing,' I responded. 'That's the whole point of hanging out.'

Mum frowned. 'But, Jerry . . . you have to do *something!'*

Just then the door swung open, and my neighbour Kramer burst inside. Kramer is *always* over here.

'Hey, Jerry! Mr Seinfeld, Mrs Seinfeld.' Kramer greeted us. He headed straight for the refrigerator.

'Hello, Kramer,' my mum replied. 'What are *you* doing today? Something, I hope. Unlike my Jerry.'

'Just percolating,' Kramer shrugged. 'Is George here yet?'

'He's right here.' I pointed underneath the table.

George has truly perfected the art of doing nothing.

'Kramer,' my dad tried, 'you must want to do *something* today . . .'

Kramer gave him a funny look. He took a huge swig of orange juice. 'But . . . I *am*. See?'

Mum just sighed.

When Elaine showed up, she was very excited.

'What's got you in such a great mood?' Kramer asked.

'I was talking to Carol from school,' Elaine explained. 'Her new baby brother is *finally* ready to meet new people. So, yada yada yada . . . we gotta see the baby!'

‘Jerry, this is wonderful news!’ my mum cheered. ‘We’ve been saying all day that you should get out.’

I rolled my eyes. ‘What’s so bad about doing nothing?’

‘Hey! I never agreed to doing nothing,’ Elaine cut in.

Dad put his foot down. ‘Jerry, listen to me,’ he said. ‘You are going to see that baby today.’

'Oh, fine. Fasten your seat belts. We're going to see the baby.' I groaned. 'Georgie-boy, wake up!'

But before we could get going, there was a knock at my door.

It was my *other* neighbour, Newman. Newman and Kramer get along great, but he is more like an archnemesis to me.

'Hello . . . Newman,' I said, glaring.

'Hello, Jerry,' he replied coldly.

'What are you doing today?' Newman asked.

I sighed. 'Going to see a baby, I guess.'

'Giddy-up!' Kramer exclaimed as he opened the front door.

'Don't forget to bring a gift!' my parents called after us.

'What's a good present for a baby?' George asked.

'Babies can't do anything,' I said, rolling my eyes. 'What are you gonna give them—an astronaut pen? What's a baby gonna do with a pen?'

Everyone had gift ideas . . .

GOLDFISH

COLOGNE

CASHMERE

CANDY

On the way to Carol's apartment, we passed Joe's fruit stand.

'Those mangos look delicious,' Kramer said.

'Kramer! We don't have time to stop,' Elaine scolded him. 'We've gotta see the baby!'

As we passed the post office, Newman turned all red with excitement.

'Let's get the baby some stamps!' he shouted.

'What's a baby going to do with stamps?' George asked.

'Can we get to the department store already?' Elaine cried. 'They'll *definitely* have a gift for the baby.'

'I've got it!' Kramer shouted. 'A puffy shirt—like pirates used to wear.'

'You want to buy *that* for the baby?' I couldn't believe my eyes.

'Jerry, it's very fashionable,' Kramer informed me.

'Come on, no-one wants to dress like a pirate,' I said.

'Well, the baby might,' Kramer insisted. 'I'll see if they have small sizes.'

I turned to Elaine. 'Elaine, tell him babies don't—'

But before I could finish, Elaine gasped.

‘It’s Puddy!’ Elaine whisper-yelled. ‘Hide!’
‘Why? I thought you were friends,’ I said.
‘He’s so chatty!’ she shrieked. ‘If he sees us, we’ll never get out of here.’

Back on the street, we all caught our breath. 'That was close!' Elaine said. 'Hey, isn't the soup place just over there?' George asked, pointing.

'But we gotta see the baby!' Elaine protested.

'I *am* kinda hungry,' I said. 'And I do like crab bisque . . .'

'Okay, fine,' Elaine sighed. 'I *do* like the bisque. But this better be quick.'

NO SOUP
FOR YOU!

'That's too bad,' I said. 'I heard the soup is stunning!'
'We could go for Chinese instead,' George suggested.
'The wait is always too long,' Elaine said.
'How about Schnitzer's Bakery?' Newman asked.

I stepped up to the counter. 'One chocolate babka, please.'
The salesman shook his head. 'All out. We only have cinnamon.'

'Cinnamon babka . . . ?' Elaine asked, confused. 'Jerry, want carrot cake instead?'

I shuddered. 'You don't make carrots into a cake.'

'Black Forest cake?' she tried again.

'Too scary,' I said. 'No way.'

Meanwhile, Kramer, George and Newman were tasting free samples.

'These pretzels are making me *thirsty*,' Kramer said, spraying crumbs everywhere.

George was trying bagel chips and dip. He dipped a chip, took a bite and then dipped again.

The baker exploded. 'Are you double-dipping?! Get out of here!'

I shrugged. 'Looks like we're finally going to see the baby.'

'I'm sorry, but you can't see the baby,' said Carol. 'He's napping.'

'Get OUT!' Elaine shouted.

Believe it or not, we were actually disappointed.

'Can't you just wake up the little guy?' Kramer begged. 'We brought a gift.'
'Thank you so much,' Carol's mum said, 'but we must let our little schmoopy rest.'
When George passed her the gift, she looked carefully at his hands.
'You have lovely hands,' Carol's mum told him. 'I'll bet you could be a hand model!'
'You think?' George gazed at his hands curiously. Then he snorted with glee.

'Well, we didn't see the baby. What now?' Elaine asked.
'We never did get food,' I reminded her.
'I could eat,' George said. Kramer and Newman nodded.

URANT
RESTAURANT

'What did you kids get up to today?' the waitress asked.

We looked at one another and smiled. Together, we answered . . .

J PETERMAN CATALOG
SELTZER
SALSA

'NOTHING!'

'The thing my parents don't get is . . . I don't have time for doing *something*! Doing *nothing* keeps me way too busy!'

MONK'S
TAXI
W 112 St